MOLLY AND THE NIGHT MONSTER

For Daisy, who sometimes used to hear
that old night monster

PUFFIN BOOKS

UK | USA | Canada | Ireland | Australia
India | New Zealand | South Africa

Puffin Books is part of the Penguin Random House group of companies whose
addresses can be found at global.penguinrandomhouse.com.

www.penguin.co.uk
www.puffin.co.uk
www.ladybird.co.uk

First published by Jonathan Cape 2008
Published by Red Fox 2010
This edition published 2018
001

Copyright © Chris Wormell, 2008
The moral right of the author/illustrator has been asserted

Printed in China

A CIP catalogue record for this book is available from the British Library

ISBN: 978–0–241–36348–5

All correspondence to:
Puffin Books, Penguin Random House Children's
80 Strand, London WC2R 0RL

MOLLY AND THE NIGHT MONSTER

CHRIS WORMELL

PUFFIN

Molly woke up in the middle of the night . . .

And heard the sound of a step on the stair.

It could have been a crocodile creeping up to catch her . . .

Or a big, brown bear, tiptoeing along the corridor . . .

Or a huge hippopotamus, stepping ever so softly . . .

Or a giant giraffe outside on the landing . . .

Or an enormous elephant, turning the door knob

and opening the door . . .

Or even a night monster come to gobble her up!

Molly threw her monster-catcher . . .

and caught the mighty beast!

Only . . .

it didn't look like a monster after all.

Molly peeped . . .

and found that she hadn't caught a monster . . .

It was a mummy she had caught!

A mummy who had come for a bedtime cuddle . . .

And a kiss good night.